D1380604

MILLY-MOLLY-MANDY'S

Friends

Other Milly-Molly-Mandy books

Family

Friends

Adventures

Schooldays

Joyce Lankester Brisley

MILLY-MOLLY-MANDY'S Friends

MACMILLAN CHILDREN'S BOOKS

First published by Kingfisher 2005

This edition published 2011 by Macmillan Children's Books
a division of Macmillan Publishers Limited
20 New Wharf Road, London N1 9RR
Basingstoke and Oxford
Associated companies throughout the world
www.panmacmillan.com

ISBN 978-0-230-75497-3

The stories in this collection first appeared in
Milly-Molly-Mandy Stories (1928)
Milly-Molly-Mandy Again (1948)
Milly-Molly-Mandy & Co. (1955)
Published by George G. Harrap & Co. Ltd

1 3 5 7 9 8 6 4 2

A CIP catalogue record for this book is available from the British Library.

Printed and bound in China

Publisher's Note
*The stories in this collection are reproduced in the form in which they appeared
upon first publication in the UK by George G. Harrap & Co. Ltd.
All spellings remain consistent with these original editions.*

Contents

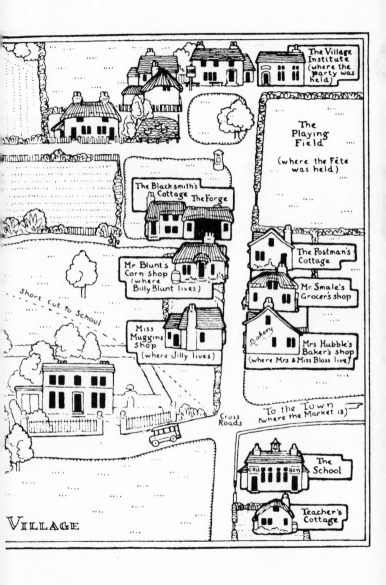

The Village Institute (where the party was held)

The Playing Field (where the Fête was held)

The Blacksmith's Cottage   The Forge

Mr Blunt's Corn-shop (where Billy Blunt lives)

The Postman's Cottage

Mr Smale's Grocer's shop

Short cut to School

Miss Muggins Shop (where Jilly lives)

Bakery

Mrs Hubble's Baker's shop (where Mrs & Miss Bloss live)

To the Town (where the Market is)

Cross Roads

GIRLS   BOYS

The School

Teacher's Cottage

VILLAGE

Milly-Molly-Mandy
Enjoys a Visit

Once upon a time Milly-Molly-Mandy was invited to go for a little visit to an old friend of Mother's who lived in a nearby town. Uncle was to take her in the pony-trap on Saturday morning on his way to market, and fetch her on Sunday evening, so that she should be ready for school next day. So Milly-Molly-Mandy would spend a whole night away from home, which was very exciting to think of. But just a day or two before she was to go, Mother received a letter from her friend to say she was so sorry, but she couldn't have

Milly-Molly-Mandy after all, as a married son and his wife had come unexpectedly to pay her a visit.

Milly-Molly-Mandy had to try very hard not to feel dreadfully disappointed, for she had never been away from home by herself before, and she had been looking forward to it so much.

"Never mind, Milly-Molly-Mandy," said Mother, when Saturday morning arrived and Milly-Molly-Mandy came down to breakfast looking rather solemn, "there are nice things happening all the time, if you keep your eyes open to see them."

Milly-Molly-Mandy said, "Yes, Muvver," in a small voice, as she took her seat, though it didn't seem just then as if anything could possibly happen as nice as going away to stay.

But while Father and Mother and

2

Grandpa and Grandma and Uncle and Aunty and Milly-Molly-Mandy were at breakfast Mrs Moggs, who was little-friend-Susan's mother, came round in a great hurry without a hat. And Mrs Moggs told them how some friends who had to go to the town on business, had offered her a seat in their gig. And as Mrs Moggs' mother lived there Mrs Moggs thought it was a nice opportunity to go and see her, only she didn't like leaving Susan alone all day, Mr Moggs being out at work.

So Milly-Molly-Mandy's mother said, "Let her come round here, Mrs Moggs. Milly-Molly-Mandy would like to have her. And I don't suppose you'll be back till late, so she'd better spend the night here too."

Milly-Molly-Mandy was pleased, and Mrs Moggs thanked them very much indeed, and they all wished Mrs Moggs a nice trip, and then Mrs Moggs ran back home to get ready.

"Where will Susan sleep? In the spare room?" asked Milly-Molly-Mandy, making haste to finish her breakfast.

"Yes," said Mother, "and you had better sleep there too, to keep her company."

Milly-Molly-Mandy was very much pleased at that, for she had never slept in the spare room – her cot-bed was in one corner of Father's and Mother's room.

"Why, Muvver!" she said. "I can't have a visit of my own, but I'll just be able to enjoy Susan's instead, shan't I? P'r'aps it'll be almost quite as nice!"

She helped to wash up the breakfast things, and to make the spare room bed, and to dust.

And then she was just looking out of the window, thinking how nice it would be for Susan to wake up in the morning with a new view outside, when what did she see but little-friend-Susan herself, trudging along up the road with a basket on one arm and her coat on the other. So she ran down to the gate to welcome her in.

And though Milly-Molly-Mandy and little-friend-Susan met almost every day, and very often spent the whole day together, somehow it felt so different to think little-friend-Susan was going to stay the night with Milly-Molly-Mandy that they couldn't help giving an extra skip or two after they had kissed each other.

Milly-Molly-Mandy took her to see Mother, and then they went up to the spare room to unpack little-friend-Susan's basket.

They put her nightgown and brush and comb and toothbrush and slippers in their proper places, and decided which sides of the bed they were going to sleep – and they found each wanted the side that the other one didn't, which was nice – though of course Milly-Molly-Mandy would have given little-friend-Susan first choice, anyway.

Then Milly-Molly-Mandy showed little-friend-Susan round the room, and let her admire the fat silk pin-cushion on the dressing-table, and the hair-tidy that Aunty had painted, and the ornaments on the chest of drawers – the china dogs with

the rough-feeling coats, and the little girl with the china lace skirt.

And while they were looking at the fretwork bracket which Father had made for Mother before they were married, Aunty came running up to say Uncle was just going to drive to market, and they might go with him if they were quick.

So they scrambled into their coats and hats, and Milly-Molly-Mandy ran to ask Mother in a whisper if she might take a penny from her money box to spend in town. And soon they were sitting up close together beside Uncle in the high pony-trap, while the little brown pony (whose name was Twinkletoes) trotted briskly along the white road.

Little-friend-Susan hadn't been for many drives. Milly-Molly-Mandy often went, but she enjoyed this one much more than usual, because little-friend-Susan was so interested and pleased with everything.

Billy Blunt was whipping a top outside his father's corn-shop as they drove through the village. They waved to him, and he waved back. And a little farther on Miss Muggins's niece, Jilly, was wheeling her doll's pram along the pavement, and called out, "Hello, Milly-Molly-Mandy! Hello, Susan!"

And then they drove along a road through corn fields, where the little green blades of wheat were busy growing up to make big loaves of bread – which is why you must never interrupt them by walking in the corn, even if you see a poppy.

When they came to the town there were crowds of people everywhere, shouting about the things they had to sell. And Milly-Molly-Mandy and little-friend-Susan followed Uncle about the market-place, looking at all the stalls of

Unpacking little-friend-Susan's basket

fruit and sweets and books and fish and clothes and a hundred other things.

Milly-Molly-Mandy spent her penny on a big yellow sugar-stick for little-friend-Susan, who broke it carefully in two, and gave her half.

When Uncle had done his business he took them to have dinner at a place where all the tables had marble tops, which made such a sharp clatter unless you put your glass down very gently. There were crowds of people eating at other tables round about, and a lot of talking and clattering of cups and plates. It was very exciting. Little-friend-Susan was having a splendid holiday.

When they had finished Uncle paid the bill and led the way back to where Twinkletoes was waiting patiently, munching in his nosebag. And off they drove again, clippety-cloppety, with

Uncle's parcels stowed under the seat.

And when they got near home it did seem queer for Milly-Molly-Mandy and little-friend-Susan to go straight past the Moggs' cottage and not have to stop and say goodbye to each other. They squeezed each other's hand all the rest of the way home to the nice white cottage with the thatched roof, because they felt so pleased.

When bedtime drew near they had their baths together, just as if they were sisters. And then Milly-Molly-Mandy in her red dressing-gown, and little-friend-Susan in Grandma's red shawl, sat in front of the fire on little stools (with Toby the dog on one side, and Topsy the cat on the other), while Mother made them each a lid-potato for their suppers.

First Mother took two well-baked potatoes out of the oven. Then she nearly cut the tops off them – but not quite. Then she scooped all the potato out of the skins and mashed it up with a little salt and a little pepper and a lot of butter. And then she pushed it back into the two potato-skins, and shut the tops like little lids.

Then Milly-Molly-Mandy and little-friend-Susan were given a mug of milk and a plate of bread-and-butter, and one of the nice warm lid-potatoes. And they opened the potato-lids and ate out of them with little spoons.

They did enjoy their suppers.

And when the last bit was gone Mother said, "Now, you two, I've set the candle in your room, and I'll be up to fetch it in ten minutes."

So Milly-Molly-Mandy and little-friend-Susan kissed goodnight to Father and Mother and Grandpa and Grandma and Uncle and Aunty, and stroked Toby the dog and Topsy the cat. And then they went upstairs to bed, hopping and skipping all the way, because they were so pleased they were going to sleep together in the spare room.

And next day, when Mrs Moggs came round to tell how she had enjoyed her trip, and to fetch Susan, Milly-Molly-Mandy said, "Thank you very much indeed, Mrs Moggs, for Susan's visit. I have enjoyed it!"

Milly-Molly-Mandy
Goes Blackberrying

Once upon a time Milly-Molly-Mandy found some big ripe blackberries on her way home from school. There were six great beauties and one little hard one, so Milly-Molly-Mandy put the little hard one in her mouth and carried the others home on a leaf.

She gave one to Father, and Father said, "Ah! That makes me think the time for blackberry puddings has come!"

Then she gave one to Mother, and asked what it made her think of. And Mother said, "A whole row of pots of blackberry jam that I ought to have in my store-cupboard!"

Then she gave one to Grandpa, and Grandpa said it made him think "Blackberry tart!"

And Grandma said, "Blackberry jelly!"

And Uncle said, "Stewed blackberry-and-apple!"

And Aunty said, "A plate of blackberries with sugar and cream!"

"My!" thought Milly-Molly-Mandy, as she threw away the empty leaf, "I must get a big, big basket and go blackberrying the very next Saturday, so that there can be lots of puddings and jam and tarts and jelly and stewed blackberry-and-apple and fresh blackberries, for Farver and Muvver and Grandpa and Grandma and Uncle and Aunty – and me! I'll ask Susan to come too."

So the very next Saturday Milly-Molly-

Milly-Molly-Mandy and little-friend-Susan set out

Mandy and little-friend-Susan set out with big baskets (to hold the blackberries) and hooked sticks (to pull the brambles nearer) and stout boots (to keep the prickles off) and old frocks (lest the thorns should catch). And they walked and they walked, till they came to a place where they knew there was always a lot of blackberries – at the proper time of year, of course.

But when they came to the place – oh, dear! – they saw a notice-board stuck up just inside a gap in the fence. And the notice-board said, as plain as anything:

TRESPASSERS
WILL BE
PROSECUTED

Milly-Molly-Mandy and little-friend-Susan knew that meant 'You mustn't come here, because the owner doesn't want you and it's his land.'

Milly-Molly-Mandy and little-friend-Susan looked at each other very solemnly indeed. Then Milly-Molly-Mandy said, "I don't s'pose anyone would see if we went in."

And little-friend-Susan said, "I don't s'pose they'd miss any of the blackberries."

And Milly-Molly-Mandy said, "But it wouldn't be right."

And little-friend-Susan shook her head very firmly.

So they took up their baskets and sticks and moved away, trying not to feel hurt about it, although they had come a long way to that place.

They didn't know quite what to do with themselves after

that, for there seemed to be no blackberries anywhere else, so they amused themselves by walking in a dry ditch close by the fence, shuffling along in the leaves with their stout little boots that were to have kept the prickles off.

And suddenly – what do you think they saw? A little ball of brown fur, just ahead of them among the grasses in the ditch.

"Is it a rabbit?" whispered little-friend-Susan. They crept closer.

"It is a rabbit!" whispered Milly-Molly-Mandy.

"Why doesn't it run away?" said little-friend-Susan, and she stroked it. The little ball of fur wriggled. Then Milly-Molly-Mandy stroked it, and it wriggled again.

Then Milly-Molly-Mandy exclaimed, "I believe it's got its head stuck in a hole in the bank!"

And they looked, and that was just what had happened. Some earth had fallen down as bunny was burrowing, and it couldn't get its head out again.

So Milly-Molly-Mandy and little-friend-Susan carefully dug with their fingers, and loosened the earth round about, and as soon as bunny's head was free he shook his ears and stared at them.

Milly-Molly-Mandy and little-friend-Susan sat very still, and only smiled and nodded gently to show him he needn't be afraid, because they loved him.

And then little bunny turned his head and ran skitter-scutter along the ditch and up the bank, into the wood and was gone.

"Oh!" said Milly-Molly-Mandy, "we

always wanted a rabbit, and now we've got one, Susan!"

"Only we'd rather ours played in the fields with his brothers and sisters instead of stopping in a poky hutch," said little-friend-Susan.

"And if we'd gone trespassing we should never have come here and found him," said Milly-Molly-Mandy. "I'd much rather have a little rabbit than a whole lot of blackberries."

And when they got back to the nice white cottage with the thatched roof, where Milly-Molly-Mandy lived, Father and Mother and Grandpa and Grandma and Uncle and Aunty all said they would much rather have a little rabbit running about in the woods than all the finest blackberries in the world.

However, the next Saturday Milly-Molly-Mandy and little-friend-Susan came upon a splendid place for blackberrying, without any notice-board; and Milly-Molly-Mandy gathered such a big basketful that there was enough to make blackberry puddings and jam and tarts and jelly and stewed blackberry-and-apple and fresh blackberries for Father and Mother and Grandpa and Grandma and Uncle and Aunty – and Milly-Molly-Mandy too.

And all the time a little rabbit skipped about in woods and thought what a lovely world it was. (And that's a true story!)

Milly-Molly-Mandy Dresses Up

Once upon a time Milly-Molly-Mandy
found an old skirt. She and little-friend-
Susan were playing in
the attic of the nice white
cottage with the thatched
roof (where Milly-Molly-
Mandy lived). They had
turned out the rag-bags and
dressed themselves in all
sorts of things – blouses
with the sleeves cut off,
worn-out curtains, old
night-gowns and shirts,

and some of Milly-Molly-Mandy's own out-grown frocks (which Mother kept for patching her present ones, when needed).

Milly-Molly-Mandy and little-friend-Susan looked awfully funny – especially when they tried to put on the things which Milly-Molly-Mandy had outgrown. They laughed and laughed.

(The attic was rather a nice place for laughing in – it sort of echoed.)

Well, when Milly-Molly-Mandy found the old skirt of Mother's, of course she put it on. The waist had to fasten round her chest to make it short enough, but that didn't matter. She put on over it an old jumper with a burnt place in front, but she wore it back to front; so that didn't matter either.

Milly-Molly-Mandy walked up and down the attic, feeling just like Mother. She even wore a little brass curtain-ring

"Let's both dress up and be ladies"

on the finger of her left hand like Mother.

And then she had an idea.

"Let's both dress up and be ladies," said Milly-Molly-Mandy.

"Ooh, yes, let's," said little-friend-Susan.

So they picked out things from the rag-bags as best they could, and little-friend-Susan put on a dress which was quite good in front, only it had no back. She pulled her curls up on to the top of her head and tied them there with a bit of ribbon.

Milly-Molly-Mandy tucked her hair behind her ears and fastened it behind with a bit of string, so that it made a funny sort of bun.

"We ought to wear coats and hats," said Milly-Molly-Mandy, "then we'd look quite all right."

So they went downstairs in their long skirts, and Milly-Molly-Mandy took

Aunty's mackintosh from the pegs by the kitchen door for little-friend-Susan, and she borrowed an old jacket of Mother's for herself. They borrowed their hats too (not their best ones, of course), and went up to Mother's room to look in the mirror. They trimmed themselves up a bit from the rag-bags, and admired each other, and strutted about, enjoying themselves like anything.

And just then Mother called up the stairs:

"Milly-Molly-Mandy?"

"Yes, Mother?" Milly-Molly-Mandy called down the stairs.

"When you go out, Milly-Molly-Mandy, please go to the grocer's and get me a tin of treacle. I shall be wanting some for making gingerbread. I've put the money on the bottom stair here."

So Milly-Molly-Mandy said: "Yes, Mother. I'll just go, Mother."

And then Milly-Molly-Mandy looked at little-friend-Susan. And little-friend-Susan looked at Milly-Molly-Mandy. And they said to each other, both at the same time:

"DARE you to go and get it like this!"

"Ooh!" said Milly-Molly-Mandy; and "Ooh!" said little-friend-Susan. "*Dare* we?"

"I'd have to tuck up my sleeves – they're too long," said Milly-Molly-Mandy. "Tell you what, Susan, we might go by the fields instead of down the road; then we wouldn't meet so many people. Look, I'll carry a shopping-basket, and you can take an umbrella, because it's easier when you've got something to carry. Come on."

So Milly-Molly-Mandy and little-friend-Susan crept downstairs and out at the front door, so that Father and Mother and Grandpa and Grandma and Uncle and Aunty mightn't see them. And they went down the front path to the gate.

But there was a horse and cart clip-clopping along the road, so they hung back and waited till it went by. And what do you think? The man driving it saw someone's back-view behind the gate, and he must have taken for granted it was Mother or Aunty or Grandma, for he called out, "Morning, ma'am!" as he passed.

Milly-Molly-Mandy and little-friend-Susan were so pleased they laughed till they had to hold each other up. But it made them feel much better.

They straightened their hats and hitched their skirts, and then they opened the gate and walked boldly across the road to the stile in the hedge on the other side.

It was quite a business getting over that stile. Milly-Molly-Mandy and little-friend-Susan had to rearrange themselves carefully again on the other side.

Then, with their basket and umbrella,

the two ladies set off along the narrow path across the field.

"Now, we mustn't laugh," said Milly-Molly-Mandy. "Ladies don't laugh a lot, not outdoors. We shall give ourselves away if we keep laughing."

"No," said little-friend-Susan, "we mustn't. But suppose we meet Billy Blunt?"

"We mustn't run, either," said Milly-Molly-Mandy. "Ladies don't run much."

"No," said little-friend-Susan, "we mustn't. But I do hope we don't meet Billy Blunt."

"So do I," said Milly-Molly-Mandy. "I'd like to meet him worst of anybody. He'd be sure to know us. We mustn't keep looking round, either, Susan. Ladies don't keep on looking round."

"I was only wondering if anyone could see us," said little-friend-Susan.

But there were only cows on the far

side of the meadow, and they weren't at all interested in the two rather short ladies walking along the narrow path.

Soon Milly-Molly-Mandy and little-friend-Susan came to the stile into Church Lane. This was a rather high stile, and while she was getting over it the band of Milly-Molly-Mandy's skirt slipped from her chest to her waist, and her feet got tangled in the length of it. She came down on all fours into the grass at the side, with her hat over one eye. But, luckily, she just got straightened up before they saw the old gardener-man who looked after the churchyard coming along up the lane with his wheel-barrow.

"Let's wait till he's gone," said Milly-Molly-Mandy. "We'll be looking in my basket, so we needn't look up."

So they rummaged in the basket (which held only a bit of paper with the money in

it), and talked in ladylike tones, until the old gardener-man had passed by.

He stared rather, and looked back at them once, but the two ladies were too busy to notice him.

When he was safely through the churchyard gate they went down the lane till they came to the forge at the bottom. Mr Rudge the blacksmith was banging away on his anvil. He was a nice man, and Milly-Molly-Mandy and little-friend-Susan thought it would be fun to stop and see what he thought of them. So they stood at the doorway and watched him hammering at a piece of red-hot iron he was holding with his tongs.

Mr Rudge glanced up at them. And then he looked down. And then he went on hammering. And then he turned and put the piece of iron into the furnace. And while he worked the handle of the big bellows slowly up and down (to make the fire burn hot) he looked at them again over his shoulder, and said:

"Good morning, ladies. It's a warm day today."

"Yes, it is," agreed Milly-Molly-Mandy and little-friend-Susan. (They were feeling very warm indeed, though it wasn't at all sunny out.)

"Visitors in these parts, I take it," said the blacksmith.

"Yes, we are," agreed Milly-Molly-Mandy and little-friend-Susan.

Then Milly-Molly-Mandy said: "Can you tell us if there is a good grocer's shop anywhere round here?"

"Let me see, now," said the blacksmith, thinking hard. "Yes, I believe there is. Try going to the end of this lane, here, and turn sharp right – very sharp, mind. Then look both ways at once, and cross the road. You'll maybe see one."

Then he took his iron out, all red-hot, and began hammering at it again to shape it.

Milly-Molly-Mandy and little-friend-Susan couldn't be quite sure whether Mr Rudge knew them or not. They were just thinking of going on when – WHO should come round the corner of Mr Blunt's corn-shop but Billy Blunt himself!

Billy Blunt noticed the two rather odd-looking ladies standing in front of the forge. And he noticed one of them pull the other's sleeve, which came right down

over her hand. And then they both turned
and walked up the lane.

He thought they looked a bit queer
somehow – short and rather crumpled.
So he stopped at the forge and asked the
blacksmith:

"Who are those two?"

"Lady-friends of mine," said the
blacksmith, turning the iron and getting
hold of it in a different place. "Lady-
friends. Known 'em for years."

Billy Blunt waited, but the blacksmith
didn't say anything more. So he began
strolling up the lane after the two ladies,
who were near the stile by now.

The lady in the mackintosh seemed to
be a bit flustered, whispering to the other.
Then the other one said (so that he could
hear):

"I seem to have lost my shopping-list, it
isn't in my basket. Have you got it, dear?"

Billy Blunt strolled nearer. He wanted to see their faces.

"No, I haven't got it," said the first one. "We'd better go home and look for it. Oh, dear, I thing it's coming on to rain. I felt a little spit. I must put up my umbrella."

And she opened it and held it over them both, so that Billy Blunt couldn't see so much of them.

He strolled a bit nearer, and stopped to pick an unripe blackberry from the hedge and put it in his mouth. He wanted to see the ladies climb over the stile.

But they waited there, rummaging in their basket and talking of the rain. Billy Blunt couldn't feel any rain. Presently he heard the lady with the basket say in a rather pointed way:

"I wonder what that *little boy* thinks he's doing there? He ought to go home."

And, quite suddenly, that's what the "little boy" did. At any rate he hurried off down the lane and out of sight.

Then Milly-Molly-Mandy and little-friend-Susan, very relieved, picked up their skirts and scrambled over the stile, and set off back across the fields. There was nobody to see them now but the cows, so they ran, laughing and giggling and tumbling against each other among the buttercups all the way across.

And by the time they got back to the first stile, just opposite the nice white cottage with the thatched roof (where

Milly-Molly-Mandy lived), you never saw such a funny-looking pair of ladies!

Little-friend-Susan's hat-trimming had come off, and Milly-Molly-Mandy had stepped right out of her rag-bag skirt after it had tripped her up three times, and they were both so out of breath with giggling that they could hardly climb over on to the road.

But the moment they landed on the other side somebody jumped out at them from the hedge. And WHO do you suppose it was?

Yes, of course! It was Billy Blunt.

He had run all the way round by the road, just for the fun of facing them as they came across that stile.

"Huh! Think I didn't know you?" he asked, breathing hard. "I knew you at once."

"Then why didn't you speak to us?"

asked little-friend-Susan.

"Think I'd want to speak to either of you looking like that?" said Billy Blunt, grinning.

"I don't believe you did know us, not just at once," said Milly-Molly-Mandy, "or you'd have said something, even if it was rude!"

"Look!" said little-friend-Susan. "There's someone coming. Let's go in quick!"

So they scurried across the road and through the garden gate. And just then Milly-Molly-Mandy's mother came out to pick a handful of flowers for the table.

"Well, goodness me!" said Mother. "Whatever's all this?"

"We were just dressing up," said Milly-Molly-Mandy, "when you wanted us to go to the village."

"And we dared each other to go like

42

this," said little-friend-Susan.

"I saw the two guys talking to the blacksmith," said Billy Blunt.

"Anyhow," said Milly-Molly-Mandy, hopping on each leg in turn, her rag-bag hat-trimming looping over one eye, "we did dare, didn't we, Susan?"

"Well, well!" said Mother. "And where's my tin of treacle?"

Milly-Molly-Mandy stopped.

"We forgot all about it! I'm sorry, Mother. We'll go now!"

"Not like that!" said Mother. "You take my coat off, and go in and tidy yourselves first. And the attic too."

"I'll run and get the treacle for you," said Billy Blunt. "'Spect I stopped 'em – they'd got almost as far as the grocer's, anyhow."

"Yes, he scared us!" said Milly-Molly-Mandy, handing him Mother's money out of the basket. "He followed us along and never said a word. He thought we were proper ladies, that's why!"

"Thought you were proper guys," said Billy Blunt, going out of the gate.

Milly-Molly-Mandy Goes to a Fête

Once upon a time, while Milly-Molly-Mandy was shopping in the village for Mother, she saw a poster on a board outside Mr Blunt's corn-shop. So she stopped to read it, and she found that there was to be a fête held in the playing-field, with sports and competitions for children, and other things for grown-ups. And while she was reading Billy Blunt looked out of the shop door.

Milly-Molly-Mandy said, "Hullo, Billy!"

And Billy Blunt grinned and said,

"Hullo, Milly-Molly-Mandy!" and he came and looked at the poster too.

"When's the fête to be?" said Milly-Molly-Mandy, and Billy Blunt pointed with his toe to the date. And then he pointed to the words, "Hundred-yard races, three-legged races, etc.," and said, "I'm going in for them."

"Are you?" said Milly-Molly-Mandy, and began to be interested. She thought a fête would be quite fun, and decided to ask Mother when she got home if she might go to it too.

A day or two later, as Milly-Molly-Mandy was swinging on the meadow gate after school, she saw someone running along in the middle of the road in a very steady, business-like fashion. And who should it be but Billy Blunt?

"Hullo, Billy! Where're you going?" said Milly-Molly-Mandy.

Billy Blunt slowed up and wiped his forehead, panting. "I'm getting into training," said Billy Blunt, "for the races."

Milly-Molly-Mandy thought that was a very good idea.

"I'm going to do some running every day," said Billy Blunt, "till the fête."

Milly-Molly-Mandy was sure Billy Blunt would win.

And then Billy Blunt asked if Milly-Molly-Mandy could count minutes, because it would be nice to have someone to time his running sometimes. Milly-Molly-Mandy couldn't, because she had never tried. But after that she practised counting minutes with the kitchen clock, till she got to know just about how fast to count sixty so that it was almost exactly a minute.

And the next day Billy Blunt stood right at one end of the meadow, by the nice white cottage with the thatched roof where Milly-Molly-Mandy lived, and Milly-Molly-Mandy stood at the other end. And when Billy Blunt shouted "Go!" and began running, Milly-Molly-Mandy shut her eyes tight so that she wouldn't think of anything else, and began counting steadily. And Billy Blunt reached her side in just over a minute and a half. They did it several times, but Billy Blunt couldn't manage to do it in less time.

After that they tied their ankles together – Billy Blunt's left and Milly-Molly-Mandy's right – with Billy Blunt's scarf, and practised running with three legs across the field. It was such fun, and Milly-Molly-Mandy shouted with laughter sometimes because they just couldn't help falling over. But Billy Blunt was rather solemn, and very keen to do it properly – though even he couldn't keep from letting out a laugh now and then, when they got very entangled.

By the time of the fête Billy Blunt was able to get across the meadow in a little over a minute, and their three-legged running was really quite good, so they were full of hopes for winning some prizes in the sports.

The day of the fête was nice and fine, even if not very warm. But, as Billy Blunt said, it was just as well to have it a bit cool for the sports. As it was Bank Holiday nearly everybody in the village turned up, paying their sixpences at the gate, and admiring the flags, and saying "Hullo!" or "How do you do?" to each other.

Milly-Molly-Mandy went with her Father and Mother and Grandpa and Grandma and Uncle and Aunty. And little-friend-Susan was there with her mother, who was also looking after Miss

Muggins's niece Jilly, as Miss Muggins didn't care much for fêtes. And Mr Jakes, the Postman, was there with his wife; and Mr Rudge, the Blacksmith in his Sunday suit.

There were coconut shies (Uncle won a coconut), and throwing little hoops (three throws a penny) over things spread out on a table (Mother got a pocket comb, but she tried to get an alarm clock), and lots of other fun.

And then the Children's Sports began. Milly-Molly-Mandy paid a penny for a try at walking along a very narrow board to reach a red balloon at the other end, but she toppled off before she got it, and everybody laughed. (Miss Muggins's Jilly got a balloon.)

Then they entered for the three-legged race – little-friend-Susan and Miss Muggins's Jilly together, and Milly-Molly-

Mandy and Billy Blunt (because they had practised), and a whole row of other boys and girls.

A man tied their ankles, and shouted "Go!" and off they all started, and everybody laughed, and couples kept stumbling and tumbling round, but Milly-Molly-Mandy and Billy Blunt careered steadily along till they reached the winning post!

Then everybody laughed and clapped like anything, and Billy Blunt pulled the string from round their ankles in a great hurry and cleared off, and Milly-Molly-Mandy had to take his box of chocolates for him, as well as her own.

Then there was the hundred yards race for boys. There was one rather shabbily dressed boy who had stood looking on at all the games, so Father asked him if he didn't want to join in, and he said he hadn't any money. So Father paid for him to join in the race, and he looked so pleased!

A man shouted "Go!" and off went all the boys in a mass – and how they did run! Milly-Molly-Mandy was so excited that she had to keep jumping up and down. But Billy Blunt presently got a little bit ahead of the others. (Milly-Molly-Mandy held herself tight.) And then he got a little bit

Off they all started

farther – and so did the shabby boy – only not so far as Billy Blunt. And then Billy Blunt saw him out of the corner of his eye as he ran, and then the race was over, and somehow the shabby boy had won. And he got a striped tin of toffee.

And Billy Blunt grinned at the shabby boy, who looked so happy hugging his tin of toffee, and asked him his name, and where he lived, and would he come and practise racing with him in the meadow next Saturday.

The next day, as Milly-Molly-Mandy and Billy Blunt and one or two others were coming home from school, they saw a big man with a suitcase waiting at the crossroads for the bus, which went every hour into the town. And just as the bus came in sight the man's hat blew off away down the road, ever such a distance. The man looked for a moment as if he didn't know what to do; and then he caught sight of them and shouted:

"Hi! – can any of you youngsters run?"

Milly-Molly-Mandy said, "Billy Blunt can!" And instantly off went Billy Blunt down the road in his best racing style. And just as the bus pulled up at the stopping place, he picked up the hat and came tearing back with it.

"I should just say you can run!" said the man. "You've saved me an hour's wait for the next bus and a whole lot of business besides."

"What a good thing you were in training!" said Milly-Molly-Mandy to Billy Blunt, as the bus went off.

"Huh! more sense, that, than just racing," said Billy Blunt, putting his hair straight.

Milly-Molly-Mandy
and the Gang

Once upon a time Milly-Molly-Mandy was in Mr Smale the grocer's shop to get some things for Mother. There was someone else just being served, so while she waited she looked from the doorway at Billy Blunt, who was spinning a wooden top on the pavement opposite, outside his father's corn-shop.

Presently some boys came along the road. As they passed Billy Blunt one of the boys kicked his top into the gutter, and another pulled his cap off and threw it on the ground; and then they went down the road, laughing and shouting to one another.

Billy Blunt looked annoyed. But he only picked up his cap and dusted it and put it on again, and picked up his top and wiped it and went on spinning.

And just then Mr Smale the grocer said, "Well, young lady, and what can I do for you this morning?" So Milly-Molly-Mandy had to come away from the door and be served.

Milly-Molly-Mandy had seen the boys before. They didn't belong to the village, but had come to stay near by, and they were always about, and always seemed to be making a lot of noise.

Well, Milly-Molly-Mandy got the things Mother wanted – a tin of cocoa, and a tin of mustard, and some root-ginger (for making rhubarb-and-ginger jam). And then she left the shop, to go across

and speak to Billy Blunt.

But as she stepped over the step the boys were coming back again, up her side of the road this time, and they bumped into her so that the basket of groceries was knocked out of her hand. The tins came clattering out, and the paper of root-ginger burst all over the pavement.

And instead of saying "Sorry!" the boys only grinned broadly and went on their way, turning back to look at her now and then.

Billy Blunt came across the road to help.

"Billy!" said Milly-Molly-Mandy, "I believe they meant to do that! They bumped into me on purpose!"

Billy Blunt said, "Lot of donkeys." And began picking up bits of ginger.

"What did they want to do it for?" said Milly-Molly-Mandy. "And pull your cap off too!"

Billy Blunt only grunted, and picked up more bits of ginger.

Mr Smale the grocer came to his door to see what was going on, and said, "Them stupid young things knocked your basket, did they? Tell your mother to give the ginger a rinse in cold water and it'll be all right. Out to make nuisances of themselves, they are. They've got something to learn, stupid young things!"

Miss Muggins's niece, Jilly, came running over. She had been watching from Miss Muggins's draper's shop opposite.

"They're a gang, they are," she told Milly-Molly-Mandy and Billy Blunt. "They try to knock people's hats off and make them drop things all the time. They've got a leader, and they're a gang!"

"They're donkeys," said Billy Blunt. And he went back to his own side of the pavement, winding up his top as he went.

Milly-Molly-Mandy said, "Thank you!" to him, and started off home with her basket. And Miss Muggins's Jilly went with her a little way, talking about "the gang" and the naughty things they did.

"They're silly," said Milly-Molly-Mandy.

"I shouldn't take any notice of them."

"Oh, I don't," said Miss Muggins's Jilly. And she went right on talking about them till they came to the duck-pond. There they parted, and Milly-Molly-Mandy went on up the road to the nice white cottage with the thatched roof, where Mother was waiting for her groceries. (She washed the ginger, and it was quite all right.)

The next morning little-friend-Susan came round to see if Milly-Molly-Mandy was coming out to play.

Milly-Molly-Mandy was just helping Mother to clean the big preserving-pan that the rhurbarb-and-ginger jam had been cooked in. So Mother gave little-friend-Susan a spoon so that she could help to clean it too! And when the pan was as clean as they could make it with their two spoons they washed their sticky hands and faces, and then Mother gave them a

big slice of bread-and-jam each to take out into the fields to eat.

So they went over the road and climbed the stile and strolled along the field-path, eating and talking and enjoying themselves very much.

And they were just turning down the lane leading to the Forge (which is always a nice way to go if you're not going anywhere special) when little-friend-Susan said, "Look at those boys; what are they doing?"

Milly-Molly-Mandy looked, licking jam off her fingers, and she saw they were the boys whom Miss Muggins's Jilly called "the gang". They were peeping round the hedge by the next stile.

"They're waiting to knock our hats off, only we haven't got any on!" said Milly-Molly-Mandy.

"Hadn't we better go back?" said little-friend-Susan.

"No!" said Milly-Molly-Mandy. "They're just silly, that's what they are. I'm going on."

So they went on, and climbed over the stile, Milly-Molly-Mandy first, and then little-friend-Susan.

And just as she had got over one of the boys jumped out of the hedge and knocked the piece of bread-and-jam (only a very small piece now) out of little-friend-Susan's hand into the dirt, and ran behind

the hedge again.

Little-friend-Susan didn't like having her last piece of bread-and-jam spoiled. But Milly-Molly-Mandy even more didn't like seeing who the boy was who did it.

"It's Timmy Biggs," she said. "You know, that boy who won the race at the Fête, and Billy Blunt used to practise with.

Why did he want to do that?"

Little-friend-Susan was looking at her bread-and-jam. "I can't eat this now," she said. "I'll take it to the ducks." (Because, of course, you never waste bread.)

So Milly-Molly-Mandy just called out, "You're silly, Timmy Biggs!" at the hedge, and they went on past the Forge and down to the duck-pond. (The blacksmith wasn't hammering or doing anything interesting, so they didn't stop to watch.)

Billy Blunt was in his garden by the corn-shop, busy with the lock of the old cycle-shed which stood in one corner. He saw them coming down the back lane, and as they didn't pass the garden fence he knew they must have turned the other way. So presently he wandered out and found them by the duck-pond.

There were five ducks quacking and paddling in the water, and little-friend-Susan was tearing her bread into as many tiny bits as she could, but it didn't go very far!

"Hullo, Billy," said Milly-Molly-Mandy, as soon as he came near. "What do you think – Timmy Biggs has gone and joined that gang. He knocked Susan's bread-and-jam into the dirt."

"I saw him with them," said Billy Blunt.

"We ought to do something," said Milly-Molly-Mandy.

"Umm," said Billy Blunt.

"Knock their caps off and see how they like it!" said little-friend-Susan.

"I don't see why we have to be silly

just because they are," said Milly-Molly-Mandy. "I don't want to be in their sort of gang."

"Might start a gang of our own," said Billy Blunt.

"Oh, *yes*!" said Milly-Molly-Mandy and little-friend-Susan exactly together. (So then they had to hold each other's little finger and think of a poet's name before they did anything else. "Robert Burns!" said Milly-Molly-Mandy. "Shakespeare!" said little-friend-Susan.)

Then they set to work to think what they could do in their gang.

"It must be quite different from that other one," said Milly-Molly-Mandy. "They knock things down, so we pick things up."

"And they leave field gates open, so we close them." said little-friend-Susan.

"And we could have private meetings in

our old cycle-shed," said Billy Blunt. "It's got a lock and key."

That was a splendid idea, and the new gang got busy right away, clearing dust and spiders out of the cycle-shed. (There were no bicycles kept there now.)

And while they were in the middle of it – sweeping the floor with the garden broom, scraping the corners out with the garden trowel, and rubbing the tiny window with handfuls of grass – suddenly they heard shouting and footsteps running. And through the fence they saw boys tearing down the road from Mrs Jakes the postman's wife's gate.

"Come on," said Billy Blunt to his gang.

And they all ran out to see what had happened.

Mrs Jakes was in her yard, flapping her hands with annoyance, her clean washing lying all along the ground.

They all ran out to see what had happened

"Oh-h-h," she cried, "those boys! They untied the end of my clothes-line. And now look at it."

Billy Blunt picked up the end of the rope, and they all tried to lift the clothes-line to tie it up again, but it was too heavy with all the washing on it. So Mrs Jakes told them to unpeg the clothes and take them carefully off the ground, so as not to dirty them any more. The grass was clean and the things were nearly dry, so they weren't much hurt – only one or two tea-cloths needed to be rinsed where they had touched against the fence.

The new gang collected the pegs into a basket, and helped Mrs Jakes to carry the washing into her kitchen, and she was very grateful for their help.

"It's not near so bad as I thought when I first saw that line come down," she said. "Do you three like gooseberries?"

She gave them a handful each, and they went back to the cycle-shed and held a private meeting at once.

The next day Miss Muggins's Jilly found out about the new gang, and asked if she could join. She wanted to so much that they let her. And they made up some rules, such as not telling secrets of their private meetings, or where the key of the cycle-shed was hidden, and about being always on the look-out to pick things up, and mend things, and shut gates, and about being faithful to the rules of the gang, and that sort of thing.

Well, they were kept quite busy in one way and another. They helped Mrs Critch the thatcher's wife to collect her chickens when they were all let loose into the road. And they kept an eye on the field-gates, that cows and sheep didn't get a chance of straying. And they rescued hats and caps and things belonging to other children when they were knocked off unexpectedly. And whenever there was anything important to discuss or if any of their gang had anything given to them, such as apples, they would go along to the cycle-shed and call a private meeting.

They liked those meetings!

One day, when they had been having a meeting, they saw Timmy Biggs hanging about by the Blunts's fence, alone. And when Billy Blunt purposely wandered over that way Timmy Biggs said to him, "I say – I suppose you wouldn't let me join your gang? I don't like that other one – I'd rather join yours. Could I?"

Billy Blunt told him he'd have to think about it and ask the others.

So he did, and they agreed to let Timmy Biggs join, if he promised to keep the rules. So he joined, and they started a rounders

team on the waste ground near the school.

Then two of the other boys took to hanging round watching, as if they wanted to join in. And presently they spoke to Billy Blunt.

"We don't like our gang much; we're tired of it," they said. "It was his idea." And they pointed to the third boy, who was sauntering by himself down the lane. He had been their gang leader.

With seven of them now they could play rounders splendidly, with Billy Blunt's bat, and Milly-Molly-Mandy and Miss Muggins's Jilly taking turns to lend their balls. The cycle-shed was too small now to hold their meetings, so they used it as a place to put the gang belongings in or to write important notices.

Not long after, just as the whole gang was going to begin a game, Milly-Molly-Mandy and Billy Blunt and little-friend-Susan began whispering together, and glancing at where the once-leader of the other gang was sitting under a tree, watching them (but pretending not to), because he had nothing much else to do.

When they had finished whispering Billy Blunt walked over to the tree.

"If you want to join in, come on," he said.

"Well, I don't mind," said the boy. And

he got up quite quickly.

They had a grand game with so many players, and they worked up a very fine team indeed.

And do you know, when, a few weeks later, the time came for those three visiting boys to leave the village and go back home, nobody felt so very pleased to see them go.

And Milly-Molly-Mandy and Billy Blunt and little-friend-Susan and Miss Muggins's Jilly and Timmy Biggs would have been quite sorry, only that now they could just manage to squeeze into the cycle-shed to have their private meetings again!

Joyce Lankester Brisley

MILLY-MOLLY-MANDY'S Family

*Once upon a time there was a little
girl. She had a Father, and a Mother,
and a Grandpa, and a Grandma,
and an Uncle, and an Aunty;
and they all lived together in a nice
white cottage with a thatched roof.*

Milly-Molly-Mandy has a very big family and she
loves them all very much. Join her as she organizes a
party for her grandparents and a surprise for her
mother, runs errands for the whole family and
steals the show at the village concert!

Joyce Lankester Brisley

MILLY-MOLLY-MANDY'S
Schooldays

On Monday Milly-Molly-Mandy
was in a great hurry to finish
her breakfast and be off very
early to school.

Milly-Molly-Mandy always has fun at school – join
her as she gets to know her teacher, makes a feathery
friend and learns lots of exciting things. Even getting
to school can be an adventure when it's raining
or snowing, but Milly-Molly-Mandy always
gets there in the end!

Joyce Lankester Brisley

MILLY-MOLLY-MANDY'S

Adventures

*Once upon a time, one Saturday
afternoon, Milly-Molly-Mandy
had quite an adventure . . .*

Milly-Molly-Mandy loves trying new things and
meeting new people. Join her and her friends as they
go on a camping trip, an outing to the seaside, meet
some amazing animals and embark on an expedition
that comes to a surprising end . . .

THE MILLY-MOLLY-MANDY
STORYBOOK

Told and Drawn by
JOYCE
LANKESTER BRISLEY

The stories of Milly-Molly-Mandy and her friends
have charmed generations of children since their
first publication in 1925. Perfect for reading aloud,
these twenty-one stories with original illustrations
will bring back happy memories for parents and
grandparents and introduce younger readers to an
enduringly popular heroine.

MILLY-MOLLY-MANDY'S
Things to Make and Do

Based on the stories by
JOYCE LANKESTER BRISLEY

Whether she's baking a cake, planting a miniature garden or having a dolls' tea-party, Milly-Molly-Mandy is always having fun. Packed with teatime treats, crafty fun and big ideas to brighten up a gloomy day, this is the perfect book for long holidays, rainy days and advetures in your own back garden!

With easy-to-follow instructions for lots of wonderful activities, including:

- ❖ Baking blackberry crumble
- ❖ Sewing patchwork
- ❖ Knitting a scarf
- ❖ Planting sunflowers
- ❖ Identifying leaves
- ❖ Building a fort
- ❖ Making a bird feeder

And much, much more!

A selected list of titles available from Macmillan Children's Books

The prices shown below are correct at the time of going to press. However, Macmillan Publishers reserves the right to show new retail prices on covers, which may differ from those previously advertised.

Joyce Lankester Brisley

Milly-Molly-Mandy's Family	978-0-230-75498-0	£5.99
Milly-Molly-Mandy's Adventures	978-0-230-75500-0	£5.99
Milly-Molly-Mandy's Schooldays	978-0-230-75502-4	£5.99
Milly-Molly-Mandy's Things to Make and Do	978-0-230-75494-2	£12.99
The Milly-Molly-Mandy Storybook	978-0-230-74407-3	£9.99
More Milly-Molly-Mandy	978-0-230-74381-6	£9.99

All Pan Macmillan titles can be ordered from our website, www.panmacmillan.com, or from your local bookshop and are also available by post from:

Bookpost, PO Box 29, Douglas, Isle of Man IM99 1BQ
Credit cards accepted. For details:
Telephone: 01624 677237
Fax: 01624 670923
Email: bookshop@enterprise.net
www.bookpost.co.uk

Free postage and packing in the United Kingdom